The Adventures of Lucas and Erythro

Written by Harry Mimna

Illustrated by Ivy O'Connor

ISBN 978-1-64191-925-8 (paperback)
ISBN 978-1-64191-927-2 (hardcover)
ISBN 978-1-64191-926-5 (digital)

Christian Faith Publishing, Inc.
832 Park Avenue
Meadville, PA 16335
www.christianfaithpublishing.com

Illustrator Ivy O'Connor

Printed in the United States of America

Note to the Reader

These stories reflect the life and experiences of blood cells as they struggle to protect the host body from harm. Teamwork is emphasized while showing appreciation for the unique function and skill of each team member. The reality of the blood cell's life cycle is touched upon.

The reader and listener can gain insight into how the blood cells function. Check out the back pages of this book and on Facebook for more "Did You Know?" bits of information to help explain background reasoning.

Enjoy reading this book and join Lucas and Erythro as they meet new friends and team members who combine their talents to combat destructive forces in their world.

The characters in this story are representations of real blood cells you have in your body! When reading *The Adventures of Lucas and Erythro*, you may notice a tiny DYK number at the end of a sentence. You can find that number in the "Did You Know?" section in the back of the book to learn more facts and information about what happens in the body!

Contents

Introduction

This book is about a wonderful team of blood cells and the adventures they come across in the body. It tells a story of teamwork to help keep us healthy.

Chapter 1
Erythro Meets Lucas

Meet Erythro. Erythro is a red blood cell whose job is to provide oxygen to all the cells of the body. Erythro thought to himself, I have the most important job of all. I pick up and deliver oxygen to all the cells in the body.[DYK1] No other job is as important as my job.

One day, Erythro noticed a strange-looking cell nearby. This cell was not nice and round like Erythro, and it had such an irregular shape that it seemed to change and move as it floated through the vessel. Erythro was curious and decided to meet this strange-looking cell.

Erythro said, "Hello. My name is Erythro."

The strange-looking cell said, "Hi. My name is Lucas."

Erythro said, "I have the most important job of all. I give oxygen to all the cells in the body."

Lucas said, "That sounds like an important job, all right."

Erythro said, "What do you do?"

Lucas said, "I float around, looking for harmful bacteria."

Erythro thought to himself, I've never seen any harmful bacteria. That must not be a very important job.

Erythro and Lucas, however, became good friends and enjoyed seeing each other from time to time.

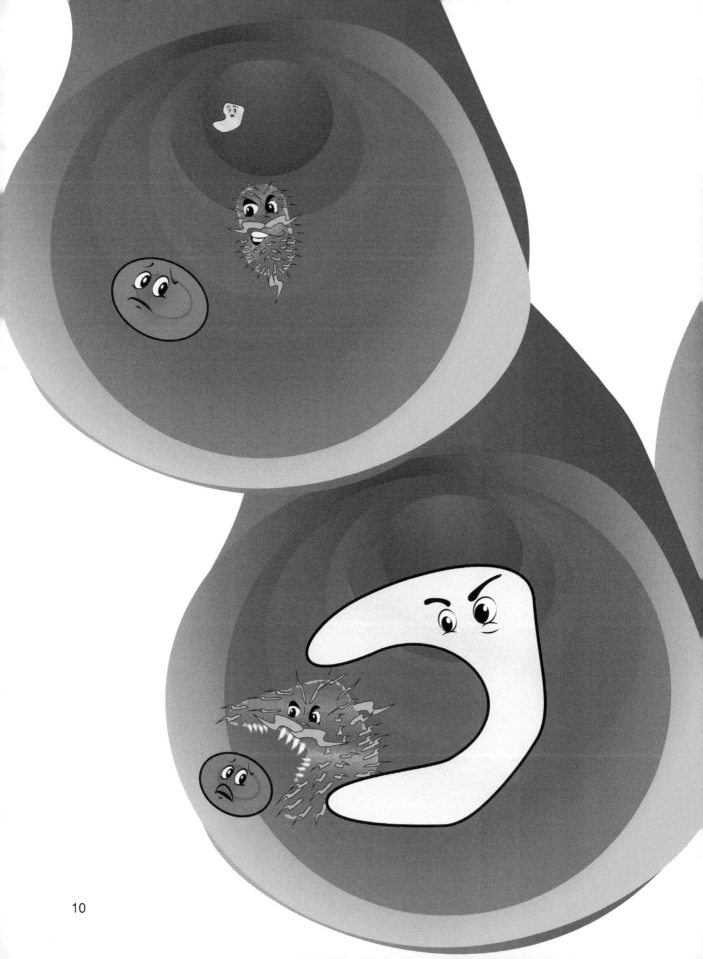

One day, Erythro was doing his important job of getting oxygen from the lungs and supplying it to the tissue cells when suddenly he saw a very large monster-like creature coming toward him. It kept coming closer and closer. Erythro wasn't able to move out of the creature's way. The creature kept coming closer and closer until it came so close it started to open its mouth, getting ready to swallow Erythro. Erythro was so scared, he didn't know what to do!

Suddenly, Erythro's friend Lucas appeared. Lucas changed his shape to grab hold of the monster-like creature and then gobbled it all up.

Then Lucas said to Erythro, "That's one of those harmful bacteria I was telling you about."

Erythro said, "Thanks, Lucas! You saved my life."

Suddenly, Erythro realized, even though he had an important job, others also have equally important jobs too.

Chapter 2
Meet Thrombo

After the incident with the harmful bacteria, Lucas and Erythro decided to resume their daily work. Erythro continued giving oxygen to the tissue cells while Lucas began searching for more harmful bacteria.

Suddenly the blood flow started to go in a different direction and began to move much faster, pulling Lucas and Erythro along with it.

"Whoa, what's happening?" said Erythro.

"Hang on!" said Lucas.

Lucas and Erythro clung tightly to each other.

"Look!" said Erythro. "Up ahead. There's an opening, and the blood flow is spilling out."

"Look out!" said Lucas. "We're going to fall through that hole!"

Just then, another blood cell jumped in front of them and plugged up the hole, stopping the blood flow, saving Lucas and Erythro from falling through.

"Hey, you're safe now," said the blood cell.

"Who are you?" said Lucas.

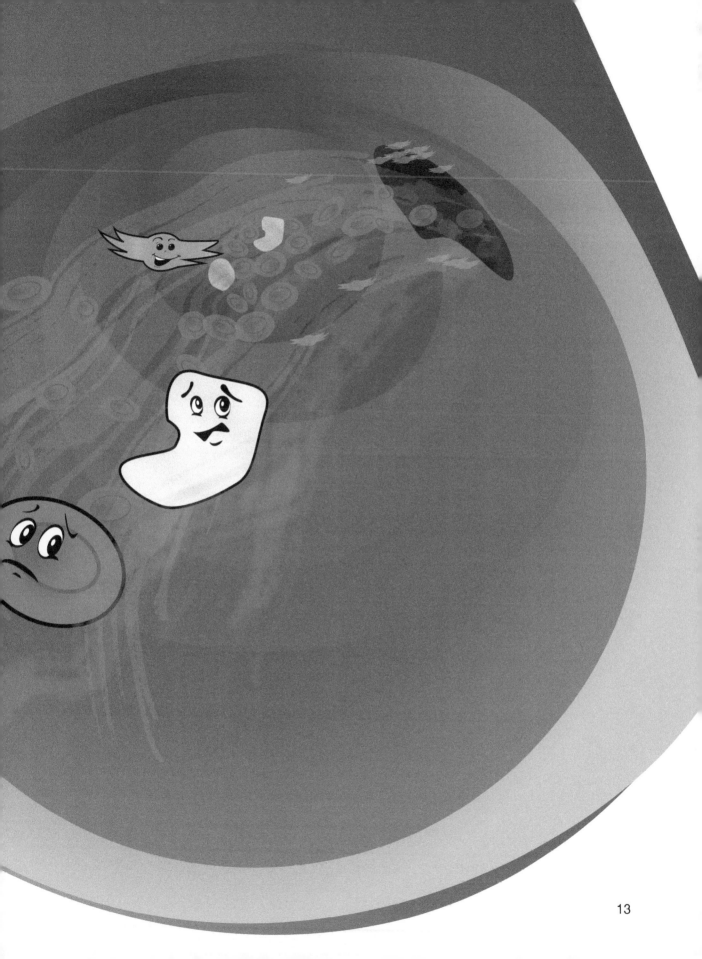

"I'm Thrombo," said the blood cell. "I blocked this hole to keep you from falling through and getting lost."

Lucas and Erythro both thanked Thrombo very much for keeping them from falling through the hole.

"No problem," Thrombo said. "It's my job."

Suddenly there was a whole bunch of other cells that looked just like Thrombo.

Thrombo said, "Meet my family. We all work together."

Then Thrombo and his family all clung together to finish sealing off the hole.^{DYK2}

Erythro realized, not only does everyone have a job as important as his, but when everyone works together, they become a team that helps each other.

Lucas and Erythro both realized, they just met a new friend, Thrombo.

Chapter 3
Lucas's Family

While Thrombo and his family were busy sealing off the hole, Lucas noticed a large number of harmful bacteria coming his way. Lucas started to gobble up some of the harmful bacteria but soon realized there were way too many for him to handle alone.

Lucas called out, "Calling all white cells. I need help fighting off all these harmful bacteria."

"Here we come," a voice called back.

Lucas turned around and was excited to see his family of white cells coming to his rescue.[DYK3]

Lucas said to Erythro, "Erythro, meet my family and relatives. They're here to help me fight off the harmful bacteria."

Erythro was amazed at Lucas's large group of family and relatives that were coming to help Lucas fight the harmful bacteria.

Lucas started to introduce his family and relatives to Erythro.

"Hey, everyone. I want you to meet my good friend Erythro," said Lucas.

"Erythro, this is Mono, Eosin, Baso, and my Uncle Neutro."

"Pleased to meet you," said Erythro.

Uncle Neutro said, "We've heard a lot about you, and we're glad Lucas has a good friend like you. Oh, and call me Phil. My friends call me Phil."[DYK4]

"Okay, I'll call you Phil," said Erythro.

"And over here is Lympho," said Lucas.

"Good to see you again," said Lympho. "Meet my children, Tecil and Becil, and our Aunt T-body."

"Nice to meet you too," said Erythro. "I don't remember seeing you before," he said with a puzzled look.

"We've seen you around before," said Becil. "We don't forget. We have a good memory."[DYK5]

Lympho said, "You don't see us very often. We hang out in the lymphatic system most of the time."

"Well," Lucas said. "Enough for introductions. We've got work to do catching harmful bacteria. Baso, help me get through some of these vessels so I can search for bacteria."

"Sure thing," said Baso.[DYK6]

With that, Lucas and his relatives set out to find and capture the harmful bacteria while Erythro continued with his job of supplying oxygen to tissue cells.

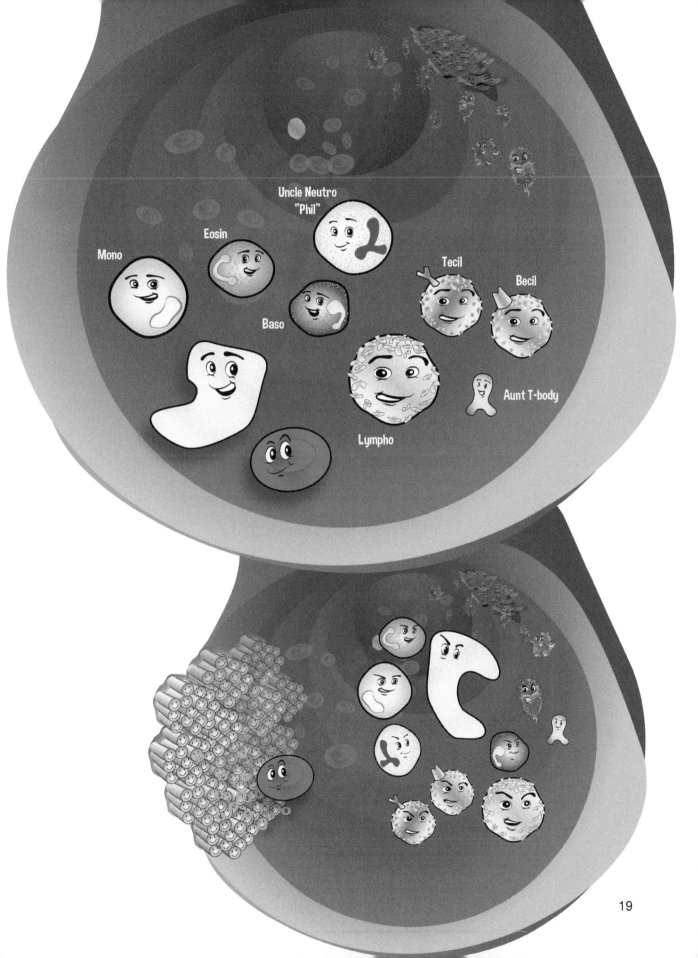

Chapter 4
Erythro Meets Erythrette

One day, Erythro was flowing along, picking up oxygen and giving it to tissue cells. Erythro also collected carbon dioxide from the tissue cells and would bring it back to the lungs. The tissue cells thanked Erythro for his job of giving them oxygen so they could continue to do their job too. Lucas came by and said hello to Erythro.

"Busy day today," said Lucas. "Gathering up a lot of debris floating around. I'll talk to you later."

"Okay," said Erythro. "Be safe."

Erythro would often say "Be safe" to his friends. It was his way of saying "Take care of yourself till I see you again."

After Lucas left, Erythro looked up and saw another red blood cell in the distance. Erythro thought to himself, this red blood cell looked much nicer than some of the others he had seen before. Erythro decided to go introduce himself.

"Hi. I'm Erythro," he said.

"Hello. I'm Erythrette," responded the red cell.

Not knowing what else to say at the moment, Erythro said, "You seem very nice."

"Thank you," said Erythrette. "I noticed a lot of tissue cells thanking you for your work."

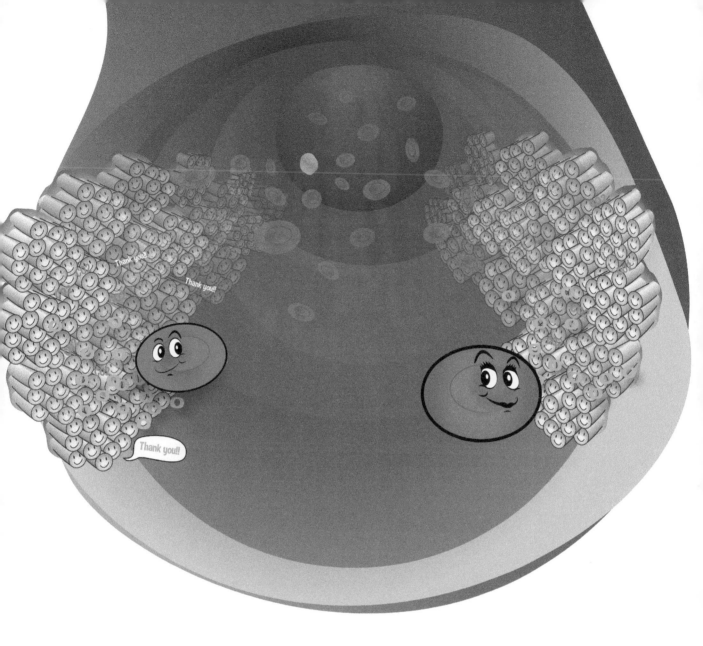

"It's nice of them to be grateful," said Erythro, "but we're just part of the team. I haven't seen you around here before."

"I just got here not long ago. New to the area.[DYK7] I haven't seen much yet," said Erythrette.

Just then Erythro remembered a favorite place he liked to go. Excitedly, he said, "Erythrette! Have you seen the Great Cavern?"

"No," said Erythrette. "I've heard about it but haven't been there yet."

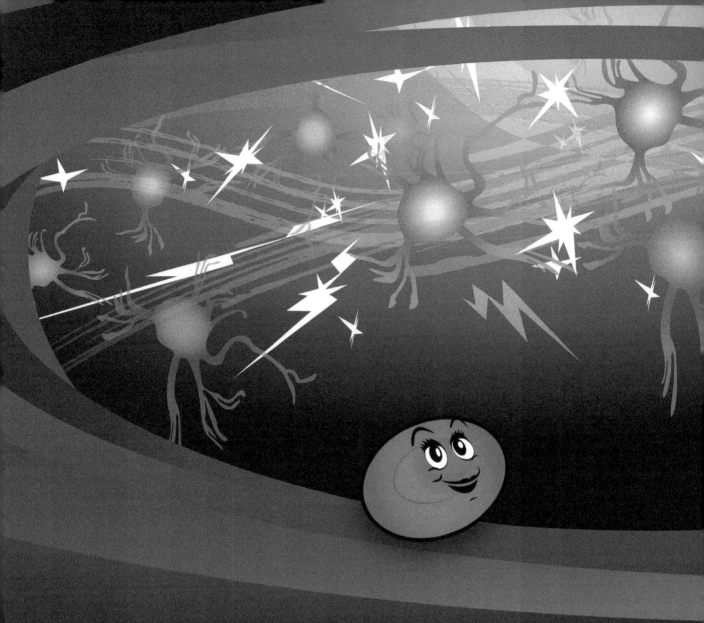

"How would you like to go there tonight?" said Erythro. "I know how to get there. I go there often. The view is extra special at night."

Erythrette agreed. That night, Erythro and Erythrette journeyed to the Great Caverns. It was a special route that was hard to find, but Erythro knew the way because he had been there many times before.^{DYK8}

When Erythro and Erythrette arrived, they found a large cliff that opened into a vast open space.^{DYK9} They sat down and listened to the gentle quiet space. Down in the lower area, there flashed a large stream of light that sounded like

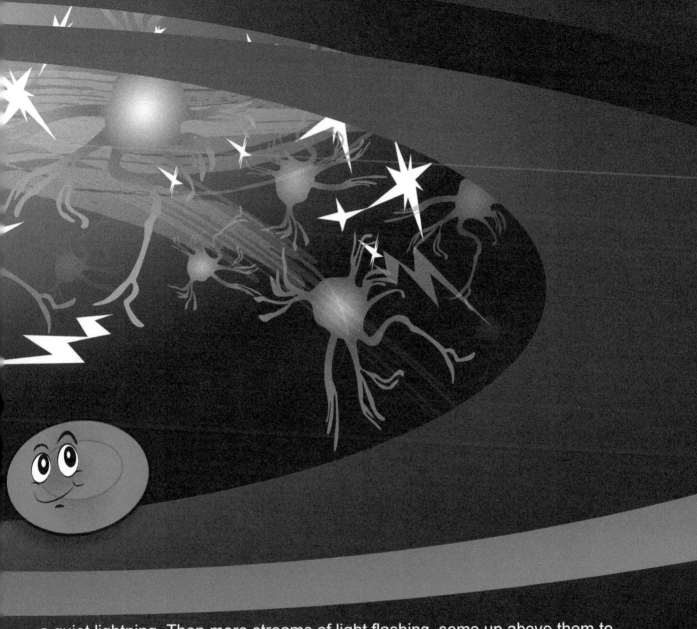

a quiet lightning. Then more streams of light flashing, some up above them to way down deep in the cavern-like spaces below. It was a spectacular site.^{DYK10}

Erythrette was glad to finally see the Great Caverns, and Erythro was glad to share his favorite place with his new friend.

Chapter 5
The Transition

One day, Lucas and Erythro were visiting with their friend Thrombo and Lucas's whole family—Mono, Esoin, Baso, Phil, Lympho, Becil, Tecil, and Aunt T-body. Everyone was enjoying visiting with each other when Lucas and Erythro started to notice a slowdown in the blood flow.[DYK11]

"We're not going as fast as we usually do," said Erythro.

"Yes, I noticed that too," said Lucas.

Suddenly, there was a very rapid blood flow in the opposite direction they had been going, pulling all the blood cells along with Lucas and Erythro.

"Look out!" said Lympho.

"We're going too fast. I can't grab hold of anything to stop us!" said Thrombo.

Suddenly, all the blood cells were pulled into a long tube.[DYK12] The blood cells along with Lucas and Erythro were flowing rapidly when all of a sudden they fell into a large pool.

The cells found themselves moving around slowly, almost in a tranquil state.

"I've never seen anything like this before," said Lucas.

"I'm scared," said Mono.

"Something tells me we don't need to be afraid," said Phil. "I have a feeling we're here for a reason."

"You mean like a special purpose?" said Erythro.

"Yes," said Phil. "I can feel it."

"Well, I'm starting to feel a little cold, myself," said Eosin.

That night, all the blood cells stayed in the pool. Even though they were cool, they felt comfortable. Erythro especially got a good night's rest. Since there were no tissue cells to supply oxygen to, he relaxed and enjoyed his time off from work.[DYK13]

That night, Eosin and Baso came over to Phil (their Uncle Neutro) and said, "Uncle Neutro, why aren't you scared like us?"

Phil said, "Well, of course I'm a little scared because this is a new experience and we don't know what is going to happen, but I try to look toward the bright side. I have faith that things can turn out well in the end. Faith is kind of the opposite of fear. It is up to us to choose—faith or fear. Your granny taught me that."[DYK14]

Eosin and Baso were glad they talked to their Uncle Neutro. They felt better and drifted off to sleep.

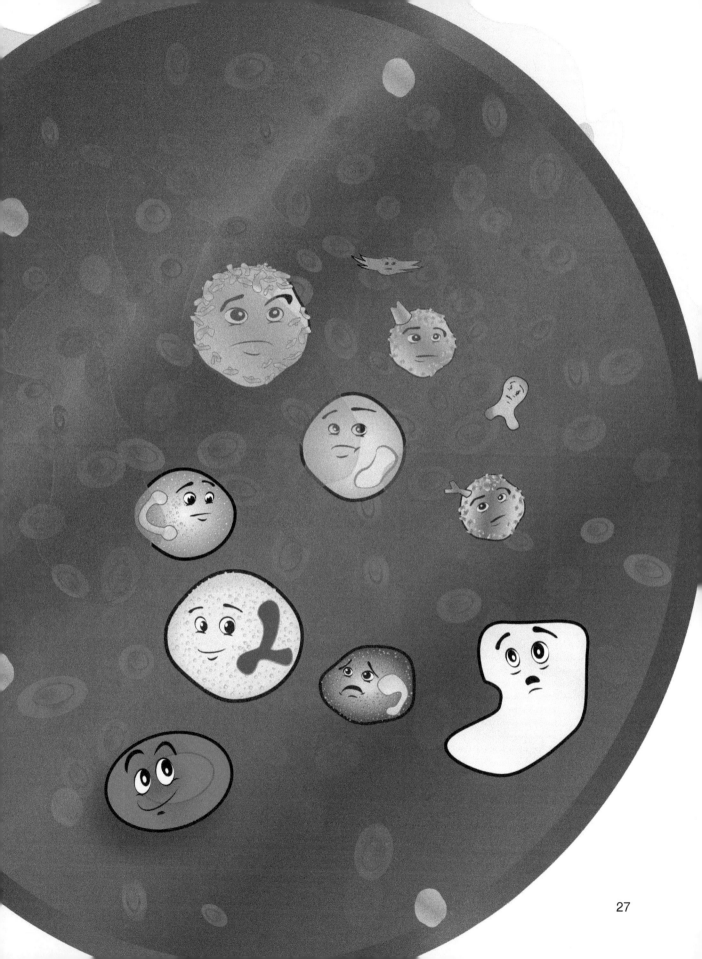

Chapter 6
A New Home

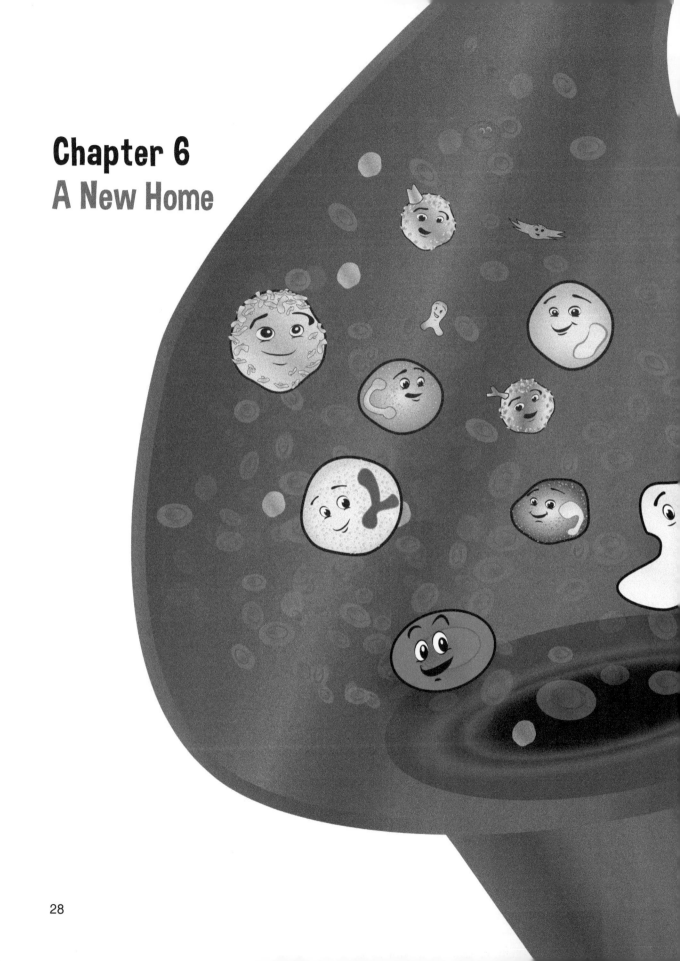

The next day, everyone woke up with a sudden jolt. The pool of blood started to flow back and forth. Lucas and Erythro were starting to enjoy the back and forth flow in the pool when the movement stopped. They looked down and saw an opening at the bottom that was slowly letting the blood cells drain out of the pool.[DYK15]

"Here we go," said Lucas.

"We'll soon find out what this is all about," said Erythro.

As they were slowly flowing down into a long tube, Lucas and Erythro met up with Lucas's family.

"Glad to see you are all okay," said Erythro.

"Likewise," said Lucas's family.

Lucas was glad his family was safe and was glad to have his family of team members with him.

"Wait! Where is Thrombo?" Lucas said, remembering a very important team member.

"I'm here," said a voice in the background.

Erythro and Lucas both looked around and said in unison, "Thrombo! Good to see you!"

"Same here," said Thrombo.

Then Thrombo, pointing to his side, said, "Erythro, I found a friend of yours."

Erythro looked over and saw Erythrette.

"Erythrette, I didn't know if I would ever see you again," said Erythro.

"Same here" said Erythrette. "It's good to see you too."

"I hate to break up our reunion, but it looks like we are about to enter a new blood flow," said Lympho.

Lucas, Erythro, and all their friends entered into a new blood flow in a new body. The vessel walls and tissues looked much like the previous body but not quite the same. Many of the blood cells and tissue cells in the new body thanked Lucas and Erythro and all their family for coming to help.

Right away, Lucas started to look for harmful bacteria and debris while Erythro and Erythrette started to give off oxygen to the tissue cells. It was like home again, but in a new home with more new friends.

Chapter 7
Team Work

Lucas and Erythro were enjoying an uneventful day in the flow of their new vascular system. Erythro was busy collecting oxygen from the lungs to give to the tissue cells, while Lucas was busy searching for harmful bacteria.

One day, Erythro mentioned to Lucas, "I hear not all bacteria are bad, that there are good bacteria doing all kinds of good for the body."

"Yes," said Lucas. "That's why I prefer to call bacteria harmful instead of bad. Some bacteria may actually be good bacteria in another environment, but in our world, bacteria can be very harmful to us."

Lucas and Erythro looked up and saw a strange-looking cell go by. It had a large number of long needle-like protrusions sticking out from its body. They looked around, and here came Aunt T-body.

"Aunt T-body, how are you today?" asked Lucas.

"I'm fine," said Aunt T-body. "I'm following that strange-looking cell. I'm trying to find out if it is harmful to us. Lucas, I'll keep you informed if I find anything out."[DYK16]

"Okay, Aunt T-body," said Lucas.

Aunt T-body continued on following the strange-looking cell. "Harmful?" asked Erythro. "But it's not a bacteria."

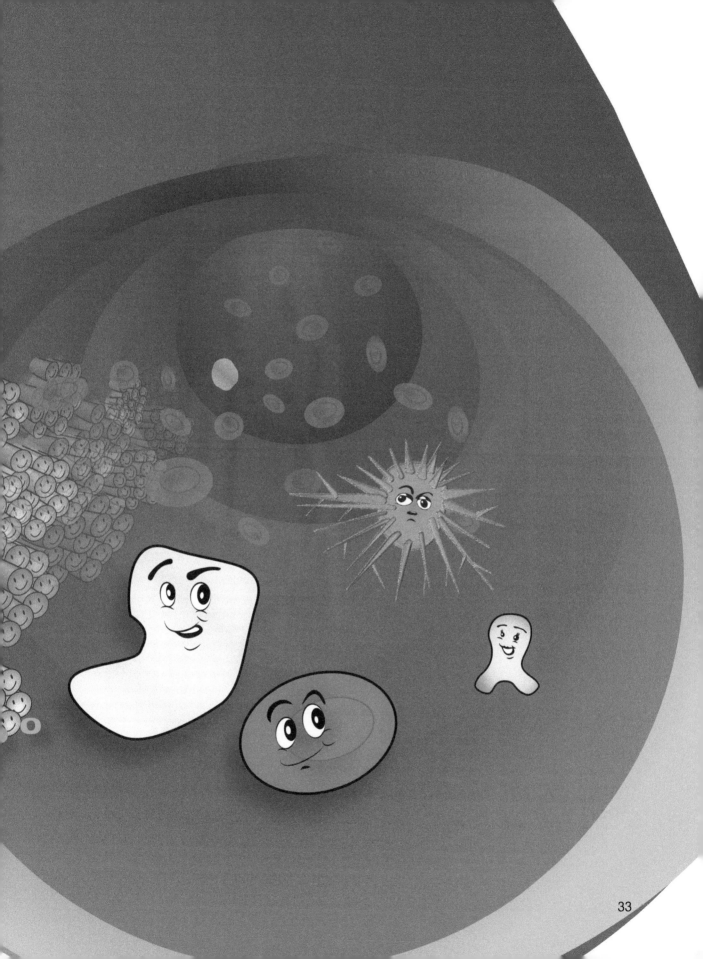

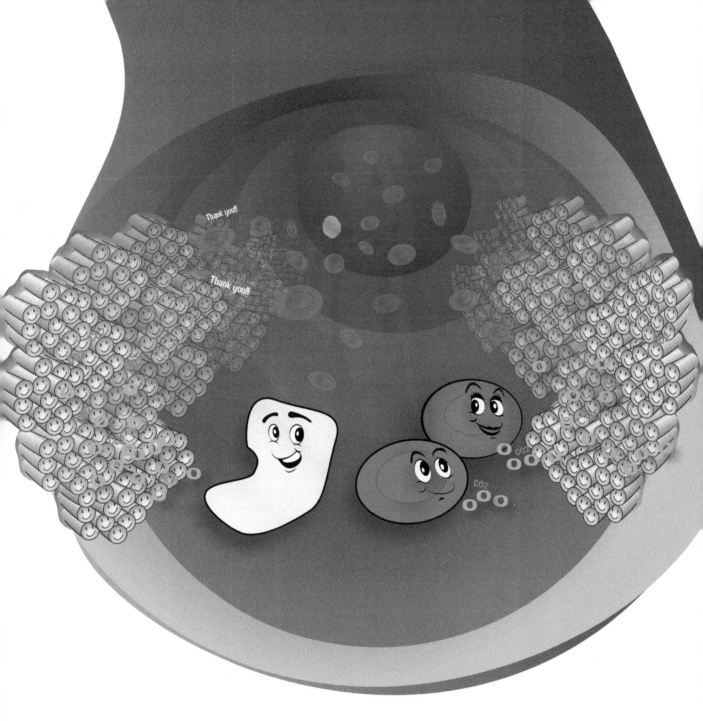

"There can be other harmful things too," Lucas responded. "I need to rely on others such as Aunt T-body to let me know what is harmful and what is not."

"Sounds like more teamwork," Erythro remarked.

"That's right," said Lucas.

Lucas and Erythro both shouted with joy at the same time, "Teamwork!" Then they laughed and laughed. They were good friends having a good time.

"Sounds like you two are enjoying yourselves," a voice from behind said.

Lucas and Erythro both turned around to see who was speaking.

"Erythrette. Good to see you," said Lucas.

"Likewise," said Erythro.

Erythrette was happy to see two good friends laughing and enjoying each other.

"Where are you going?" asked Erythro.

"I'm running low on hemoglobin," responded Erythrette.[DYK17] "Headed for the digestive system to try and find some iron."

Lucas looked confused and turned to Erythro. "Iron?" asked Lucas.

"Yes," said Erythro. "Iron helps build up our hemoglobin, which is a tool that helps us red cells carry more oxygen and deliver it to other cells. I am going to go with Erythrette. My hemoglobin is getting low too."

"Okay," said Lucas.

Erythrette and Erythro headed for the digestive system while Lucas continued his job of looking for harmful bacteria and other things harmful to the body.

Chapter 8
The Tumor

One day, Erythro was supplying oxygen to the tissue cells when he came across a large group of cells that grabbed some oxygen away from Erythro as he passed by. The large group of cells seemed to stay to themselves. They did not show any appreciation to Erythro even though he allowed them to have some oxygen. Erythro went over to some other nearby tissue cells to supply oxygen to them.

"What's with that group of cells? They didn't seem very polite when they took away some of my oxygen. They seemed to ignore me," said Erythro.

"They mostly stay to themselves and ignore us too," said a tissue cell. "They are called tumor cells. They keep taking food and oxygen, and sometimes, there is not enough food and oxygen for us until more of you red blood cells come by."

"They grow faster in number than the rest of us," said another tissue cell.

"I'm curious," Erythro said, as he started to go closer to the tumor cells to ask them what they were doing here.

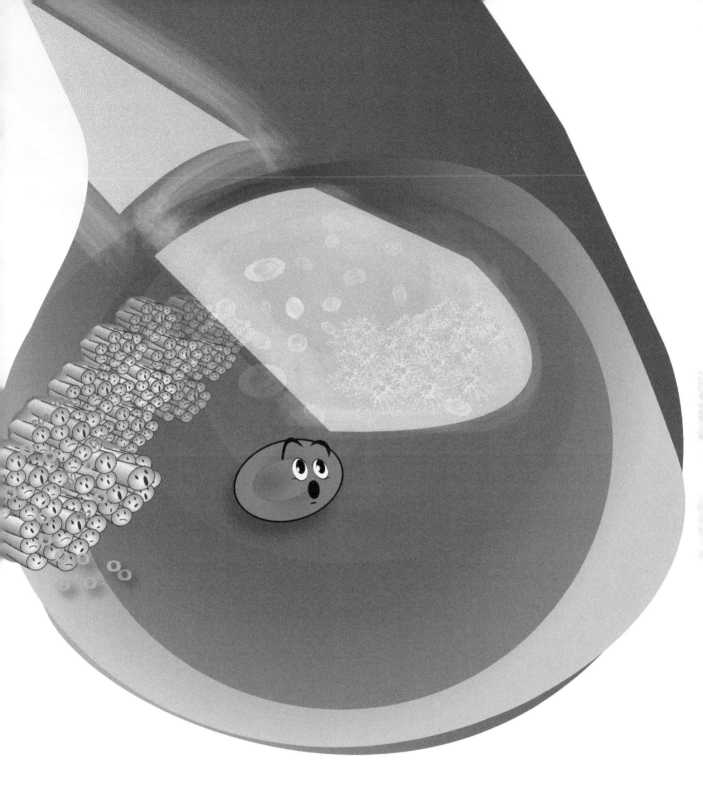

"Look out!" a tissue cell suddenly called out. "Jump back!" said another. Erythro jumped back just in time to see a large beam of light flash in front of him. Erythro moved farther away from the tumor cells.

"Whoa! That was close!" Erythro said to the tissue cells. Suddenly, there were more flashes of light directed at the tumor cells. When the light flashes stopped, the tumor cells began to move slower but still ignored Erythro and the other tissue cells.

"Well, I'm running low on oxygen," said Erythro, "but I'll be back tomorrow to give you more oxygen. In the meantime, there should be more red blood cells coming by soon to supply you with more oxygen."

The tissue cells thanked Erythro as he continued on his journey back to the lungs to pick up more oxygen.

The next day, Erythro was returning to the tissue cells that were near the tumor cells. He had a full load of oxygen and was looking forward to supplying the tissue cells with much-needed oxygen. He was wondering if the tumor cells would try to grab more oxygen from him. Erythro decided he would try to keep a distance from the tumor cells until he could reach the tissue cells first to supply them with oxygen.

When Erythro arrived, he found the tumor cells shriveled up and some of the tumor cells broken into pieces. He looked over and saw his good friend Lucas along with Lympho and Phil. They were busy collecting the shriveled tumor cells and debris that was floating around.

"There you are," said Lucas. "Good to see you again. As you can see, my family and I are busy cleaning up the effects of the radiation beams from yesterday."

"So *that's* what it was," said Erythro. "Radiation beams."

"Yes," said Lucas, "and I'm grateful to your tissue cell friends for warning you just in time to keep you from getting hit by those radiation beams. They told me about your experience yesterday."

Lympho came by to greet Erythro while Erythro and Lucas were talking.

"Erythro, I'm glad you are all right!" said Lympho. Then he turned to Lucas and said, "Lucas, once we get this debris cleaned up, there will be no more tumor cells in this area."

"Yes," said Lucas. "It looks like the radiation beams were successful in eliminating these tumor cells."

Erythro went over to the tissue cells and thanked them again for helping to keep him safe.

"That's okay," said the tissue cells. "Guess that makes us part of your team!"

"It sure does," said Erythro. "It sure does."

Chapter 9
Viral Invasion

One day Erythro was busy collecting oxygen in the lungs and distributing it to the tissue cells, as he usually does. This day, however, Erythro noticed he was having difficulty collecting a full load of oxygen to take to the tissue cells. He had plenty of hemoglobin, which helps him gather oxygen, so he knew that was not the problem. He was feeling a little tired too. Some of the tissue cells started to complain of not getting enough oxygen. "We need more oxygen!" they said.

"Yes, I know," responded Erythro. "I'm having difficulty finding enough oxygen to bring to you. I'll keep doing the best I can."

"We know you will," said the tissue cells. "We're glad for your help."

Erythro found Erythrette, and she, too, was having the same problem getting enough oxygen from the lungs to supply the tissue cells.

Lucas came by to see how Erythro was doing. Lucas said to Erythro, "How are you doing, Erythro? Something is wrong in the body, but I haven't been able to figure it out yet."

Erythro said, "I'm a little weak, but I'll manage."

Just then, Becil came by. Becil had a strong grip on a cell that did not look healthy.[DYK18] "Lucas," cried Becil, "I've been looking for you! I need you to take care of this cell. It looks like a virus has entered the cell and is making it sick."[DYK19]

"So *that's* it," said Lucas. "A viral infection. There will be too many sick cells to take care of myself. Becil, where is Lympho? We need his help."

"Lympho's not here yet but will come when he gets enough help to fight the virus," responded Becil. "In the meantime, we'll have to fight the virus ourselves."[DYK20]

"Okay, let's go!" said Lucas, turning to Erythro as he started off. "Take care, Erythro. I know you and Erythrette will do the best you can to supply oxygen to the cells."

"Be safe," said Erythro to Lucas.

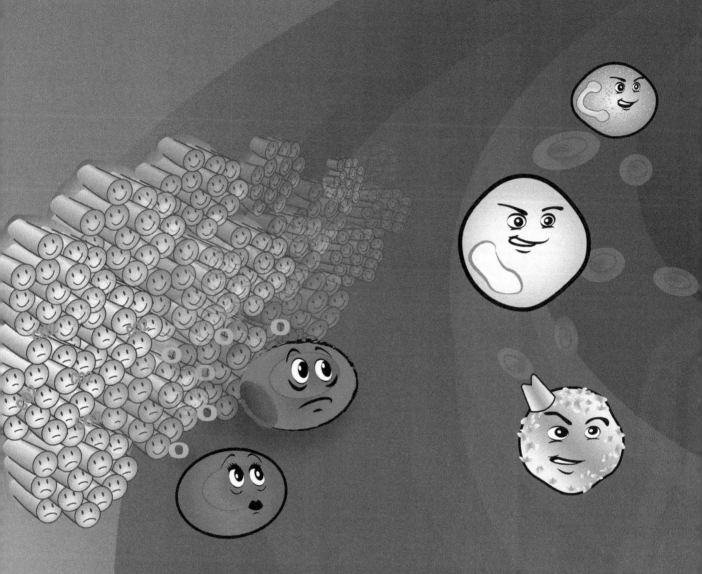

Lucas headed off and devoured the sick cell that had the virus inside. Then he followed Becil, and when Becil found another cell that was infected with the virus, Becil would grab hold of that cell until Lucas could come and devour it.

In the meantime, Erythro was busy trying to supply oxygen to all the tissue cells, giving them as much oxygen as he could. He was getting weaker but tried to ignore it.

Suddenly, Erythro slipped and fell along the wall but got back up. His side was injured and sore. He felt like quitting, but he had to keep going! He had to keep carrying oxygen to the cells to keep them alive!

Lucas had spotted a virus and was going after it when he saw Lympho coming out of the lymphatic system. Lucas cheered with joy when he saw Lympho and a whole army of white cells ready to fight the virus. Lympho and his army immediately began going after any virus they saw and eating them up along with the infected cells.

The battle lasted a long time, but in the end, the virus infection had been defeated. Then Erythro, Erythrette, and all the red blood cells were able to collect enough oxygen and restore oxygen levels to the tissue cells.

Chapter 10
Goodbye and Hello

Erythro still had his injury from the last battle with the virus but was moving along as best he could. His job of giving oxygen to the tissue cells was getting harder to do. Erythrette noticed from a distance, Erythro's difficulty in moving. She wished she could help but knew there was nothing she could do.

Lucas came by to see Erythro. "How are you doing Lucas?" said Erythro.

"Just like you," said Lucas, "doing the best I can. Haven't been feeling so good lately. Think I've got my fill of eating up bacteria and viruses. I don't think I can handle many more."[DYK21]

Erythro looked up at Lucas. Lucas seemed filled with extra debris and bacteria, more than usual. Erythro said, "My injury doesn't seem to be improving, but you're right, I'm doing the best I can."

Erythro paused for a moment, then he said, "Lucas, we've had good times and great adventures together."

Lucas said, "Yes, we have. We certainly gave life a whirl. I'm glad we've been friends through so many adventures."

There was another silent pause between them. Then Lucas continued, "Erythro, I'm going to the lymphatic system to visit my family. I'd like you to come along."

"I'd like that," said Erythro.

Lucas wrapped himself around Erythro to help him along. As they got to the lymphatic system, Lympho was there to greet them. Then they disappeared into the lymphatic system.[DYK22]

Erythrette watched as they left. She felt grateful to have experienced a part of their friendship and many of their adventures together. Erythrette was proud of them for all the work they had done.

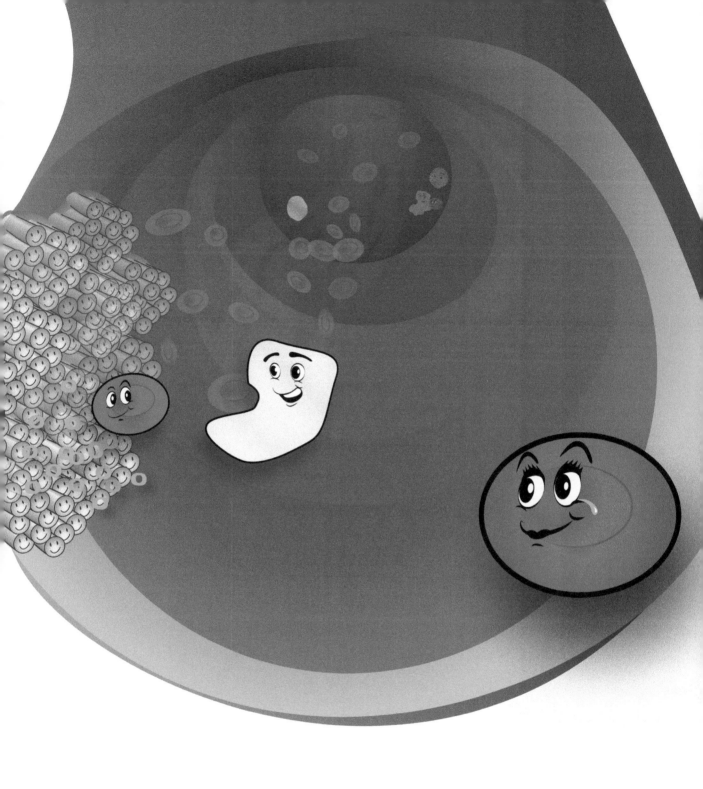

Just then, Erythrette's attention was drawn to a red cell and white cell in the distance. They were youthful and energetic-looking. Not noticing the other at first, they suddenly bumped into each other.

"Whoa! Excuse me," said the white cell. "Didn't mean to bump into you."

"That's okay," said the red cell. "What's your name?"

"I'm Lucas the Second, but you can just call me Lucas," said the white cell. "What is your name?"

"My name is Erythro the Second, but you can call me Erythro, and I have the most important job in all the world. I supply oxygen to all the tissue cells of the body."

"That's interesting," said Lucas. "I thought I had the most important job in all the world. I look for harmful bacteria and gobble them up so they don't hurt anyone."

Erythro and Lucas both looked at each other for a moment, and then they both laughed and laughed and laughed.

Erythrette watched the young Lucas and Erythro as they seemed to be developing an almost instant friendship for each other. A tear came to her eye. Erythrette didn't know if it was a sad tear because of her friends Lucas and Erythro leaving or a joyful tear in seeing the new friendship growing between the young Lucas and Erythro. Either way, she cherished the tear as she watched the young friends travel down the stream on their next new adventure.

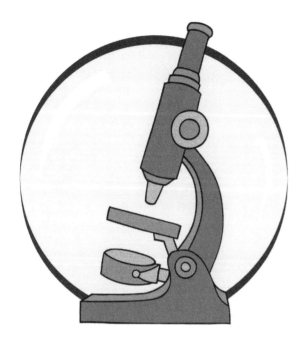

Did You Know?

Science behind the Scenes

The characters in this story are representations of blood cells you have in your body! When reading *The Adventures of Lucas and Erythro*, you may have seen a tiny DYK number at the end of a sentence. You can find that number in this "Did You Know?" section to learn more facts and information about what happens in the body!

Chapter 1

1. Blood cells and fluid travel through the body in vessels called the circulatory system. The circulatory system is made up of the vascular system (which is where most of the blood circulates) and the lymphatic system.

Chapter 2

2. Thrombocytes (Thrombo and his family) become sticky during a stressful time in the body. This helps thrombocytes cling together forming a blood clot.

Chapter 3

3. Leukocytes (Lucas) represent many different kinds of white blood cells, many of which have special functions in helping the body defend against foreign invasion.

4. Neutraphils (Uncle Neutro [a.k.a. Phil]) are the most abundant in the category of white cells called granulocytes. (See note 14 on granulocytes.)

5. T cells (Tecil) and B cells (Becil) are also called memory cells. They can remember pathogens from the past in case that pathogen returns to invade the circulatory system. (See note 16 on pathogens.)

6. One of the functions of basophils (Baso) is to secrete a chemical (histamine) that dilates (makes larger) the smaller vessels so other white blood cells can get through.

Chapter 4

7. Blood cells are manufactured in the bone marrow. Once matured, they are introduced into the blood stream.

8. This can represent what is called the blood-brain barrier. This barrier system prevents unwanted material from getting into the brain. There are just a few areas in the brain that do not have the blood-brain barrier.

9. This location is an open area in the brain called a ventricle. To a microscopic blood cell, this area would appear to be a vast open space.

10. The lightning flashes represent the electrical space (called synapse) between the nerve endings (dendrites). Whether there is actually a visible flash is questionable.

Chapter 5

11. When a tourniquet, a tightened band around the arm, is placed on the arm, it slows down the blood flow.

12. This represents what happens when someone is donating blood.

13. After donating blood, the blood is stored in a bag and refrigerated until ready for use. Several tests are done to determine safety of use. Often blood is separated into different parts, such as plasma (the fluid without the cells), packed cells (blood cells with most of the plasma removed), and platelets (another name for thrombocytes). There can be other variations of blood transfusions too. In this case, however, where there is no separation of blood parts, this is called whole blood transfusion.

14. *Granny* is a pun on granulocytes. Eosinophils, basophils, neutrophils, and monocytes are classified as granulocytes. They have a granular appearance when looked at in the microscope.

Chapter 6

15. When taken out of the refrigerator, blood is kneaded (mixed) and then hung up to be slowly transfused.

Chapter 7

16. Antibodies (Aunt T-body) are designed to search for and identify possible harmful pathogens, like bacteria, viruses, and abnormal-looking cells and then connect to the pathogen to alert white cells which can come and destroy the pathogen.

17. Hemoglobin is a protein found in red cells that hold the oxygen molecules while red cells are transporting the oxygen.

Chapter 9

18. B cells also attach to cells that are considered harmful, and this signals white cells to come and destroy the harmful cell.

19. A virus can enter into a cell through its cell wall and hide to keep from being detected. This virus will then reproduce inside the cell. When the cell dies, the viruses will leave that cell and enter into other cells to repeat the process over again.

20. Once the virus is detected, lymphocytes (Lympho) begin reproducing in large numbers in the lymphatic system. However, the lymphocytes will not enter the vascular system until there are enough white cells to fight the virus. This can take one to two days. That leaves the small number of white cells already in the vascular system to fight the virus alone until additional help arrives.

Chapter 10

21. The job of the white cell is to ingest infectious material and debris. When the white cell gets filled, it will not survive much longer. Its job is done and other white cells come in to resume the work.

22. When a blood cell's life is over, lymphocytes digest many of the cells and deposit some of the cells ingredients for recycling back into the body. Remaining waste material gets disposed of through many of the body's waste disposal methods.

TAKE A CLOSER LOOK!

About the Author

Harry Mimna grew up in a small town in the mountains of Pennsylvania. He went to work as a nursing assistant in the 1960s during a military draft. The nurses he worked with encouraged him to go into nursing as a career since he did a great job. So as the first person in his family to go to college, he received his associate degree in nursing in 1976 and his bachelor of science degree in 1980 at the University of Maryland. His first job as a registered nurse was at Johns Hopkins Hospital. He enjoyed a long and fulfilling career as an RN at many different hospitals. He retired from nursing after thirty-eight years in 2014. While he worked as a nurse, he also married and had two daughters, whom he would tell made-up bedtime stories to. The stories were of these two cells named Lucas and Erythro, who would go on many different adventures in the body. His two daughters would sit starry-eyed and attentive at their dad's stories and would ask for a new story every night.

His oldest daughter, Ivy, now grown, fondly remembered her favorite childhood stories of Lucas and Erythro. She often asked that he write down the stories she was told as a child. She didn't want the stories to be forgotten. She wanted to one day read the stories to her own children. It wasn't until Harry retired that he finally took the time to write his stories down, and the book, *The Adventures of Lucas and Erythro* was born.

As an experienced graphic designer, his daughter, Ivy, jumped at the opportunity to illustrate and design the book, make her favorite childhood stories come to life, and share these stories with other children around the world.

CPSIA information can be obtained
at www.ICGtesting.com
Printed in the USA
BVHW02s1658130918
527344BV00006B/22/P